COLORING & ACTIVITY BOOK

bendon®

THE BENDON name, logo and
Tear and Share are trademarks of
Bendon, Ashland, OH 44805.

DRAW

The Country Western
Trolls have four legs!

Draw a picture of yourself
as a four-legged Troll!

Secret Message

Use the key to decipher the secret message.

Interlock

Complete the puzzle by using the words from the list.

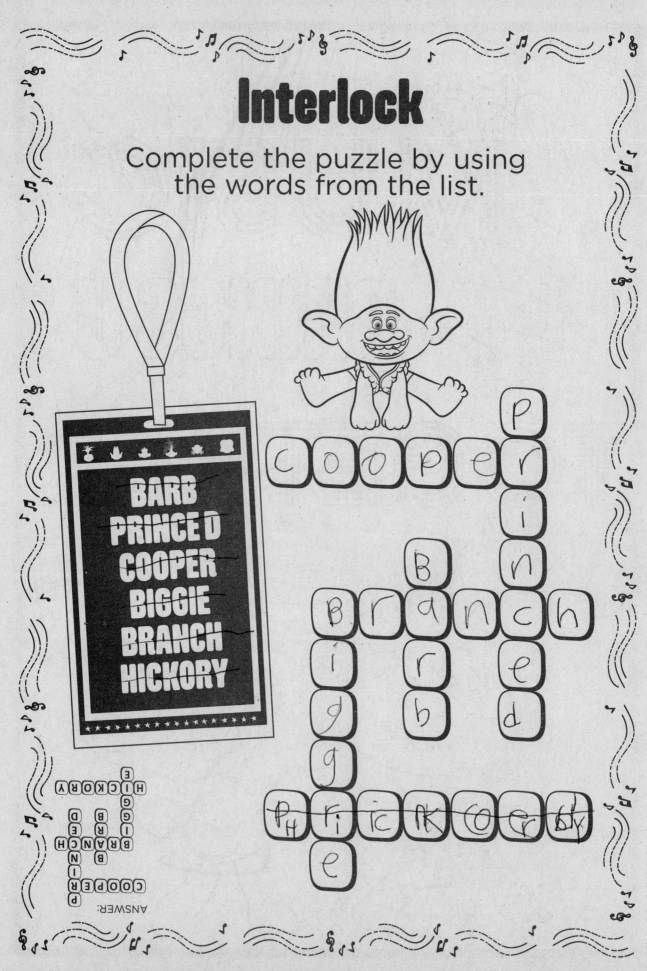

BARB
PRINCE D
COOPER
BIGGIE
BRANCH
HICKORY

Dot-to-Dot

Go dot-to-dot to see what King Peppy is holding!

THE ADVENTURE AWAITS

Which Path?

Which path leads
Poppy to Queen Barb?

A

B

C

Your
Answer

MISSING PIECE

Find the missing piece of the image and finish the drawing of Hickory!

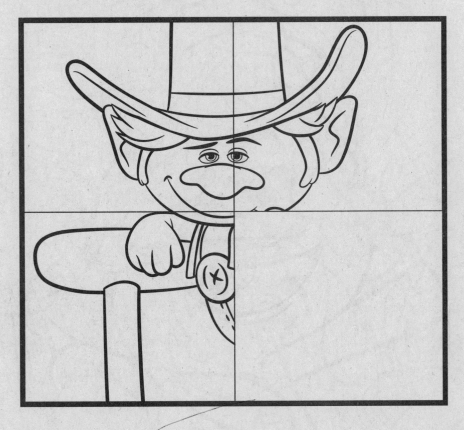

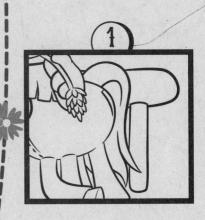
1

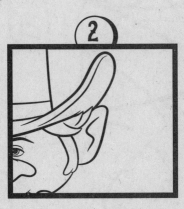
2

3

A-MAZE-ING JOURNEY

Help Queen Poppy find King Trollex!

START

FINISH

ANSWER:

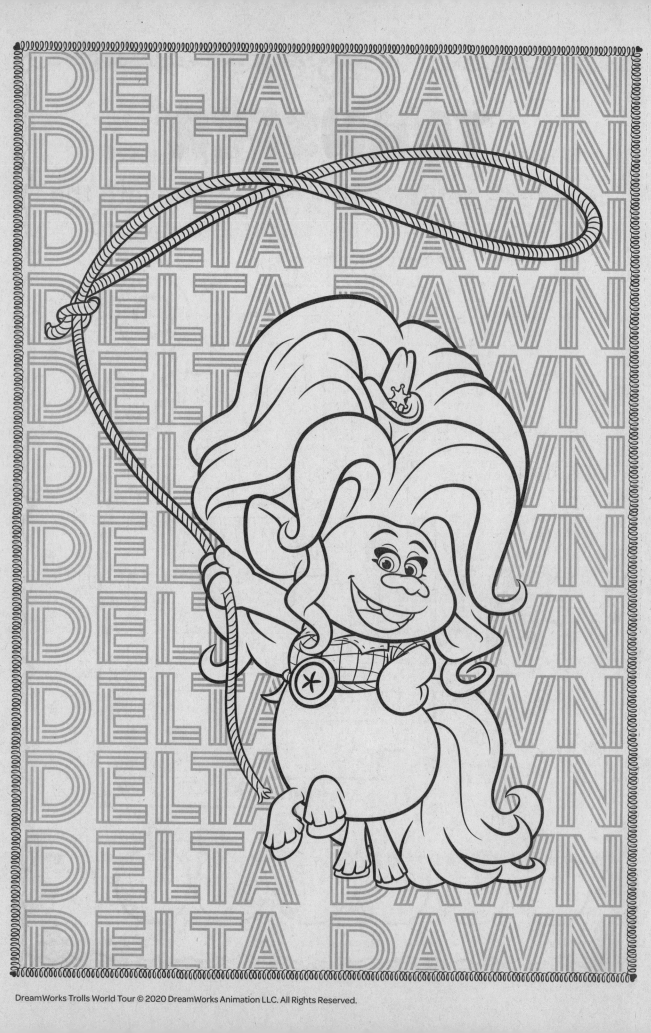

TRANSFER

Using the paths, transfer the letters into the circles below to unscramble the word.

E P O R C O

C O O P E R

LET'S DRAW!

Trace the gray lines to finish
the drawing of Queen Barb!

How many words can you make from the letters in the phrase below?

The More Trolls the Merrier

Find Fourteen

Look forward, backward, up, down, and diagonally to find the word below 14 times.

DANCE

```
D A N C E E C N A D
A A D E C C N A D A
N E C C N N A D A N
C A E A A A D A N C
E C N A D D D A N C E
D N A C E A N C E N
A A D D A N C E A N
N C N A N C E C A A
D A N C E E N C E D
```

Which is Different?

Which picture of Cloud Guy is different from the others?

Count 'Em Up

How many cactuses do you see?

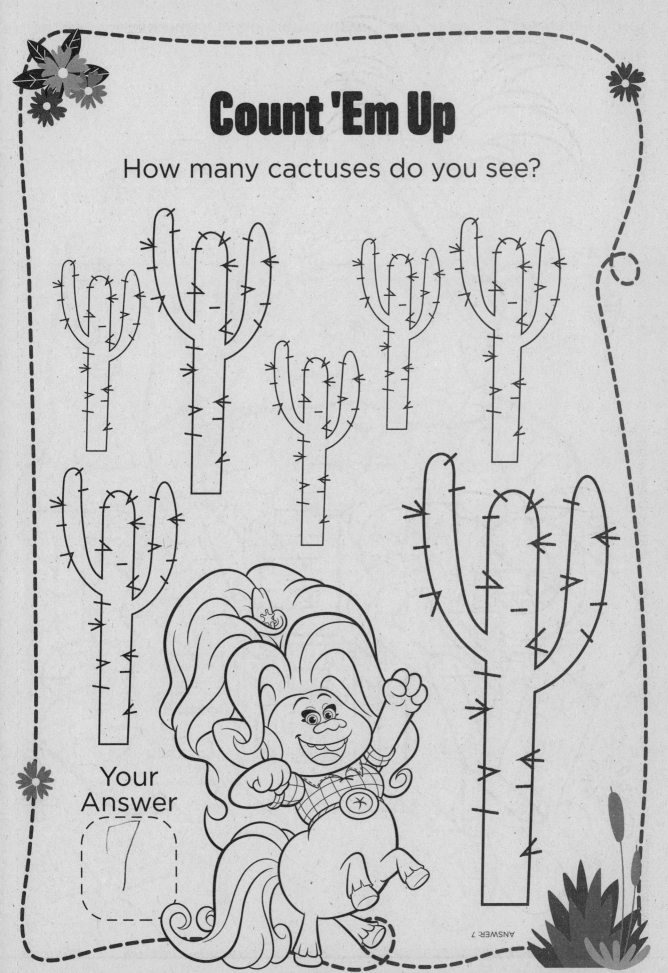

Your Answer

7

UNSCRAMBLE

Unscramble the words listed below.

_____   _____
ALDET   WADN

_____
ERSTENW

_____
TRUCONY

_____
CHRIKOY

_____   _____
UORF   SGLE

ANSWER: DELTA DAWN, WESTERN, COUNTRY, HICKORY, FOUR LEGS

Troll Match

Which two pictures of Cooper are the same?

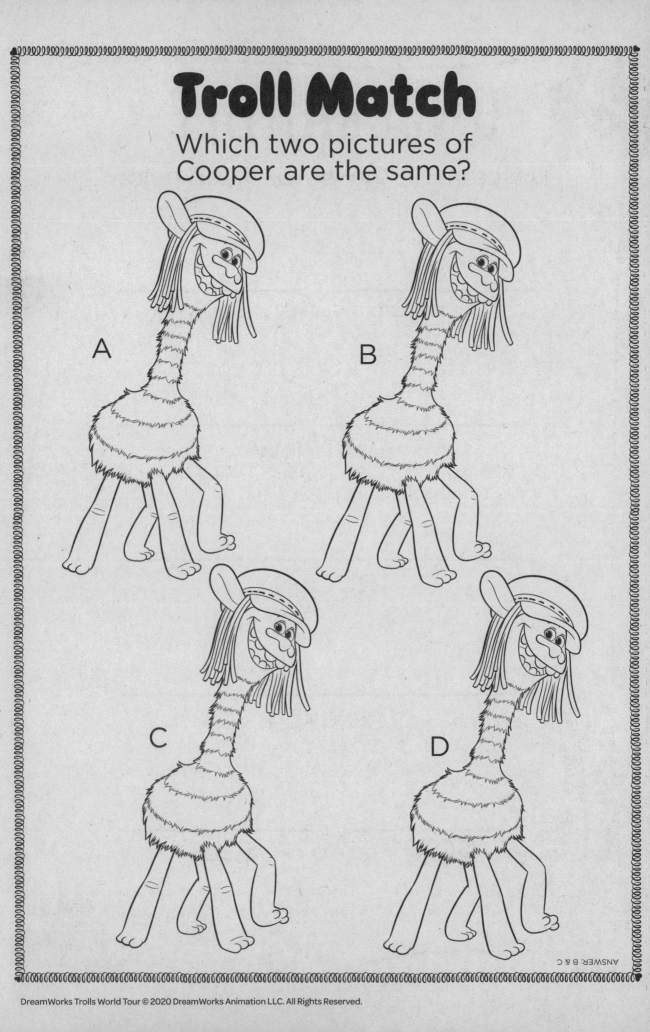

A

B

C

D

ANSWER: B & C

SQUARES

Taking turns, connect a line from one star to another. Whoever makes the line that completes the square puts his or her initial in the square. The person with the most squares at the end of the game wins!

TIC-TAC-TOE

Play a game of Tic-Tac-Toe with a friend!

Follow the Path

Find your way through the puzzle by following the word **T-E-C-H-N-O-R-E-E-F** in order.

START

```
T O G P C H N T F C
E M F T E B O D Q J
C S E W G Y R E E F
H C E K B U K N L T
N O R X H O N H C E
I V D H P R A J Y L
C E T F E E N T R A
H A S Z O I F V X E
N O R E E F M U E R
```

FINISH

Shadow Match
Which shadow matches Cooper?

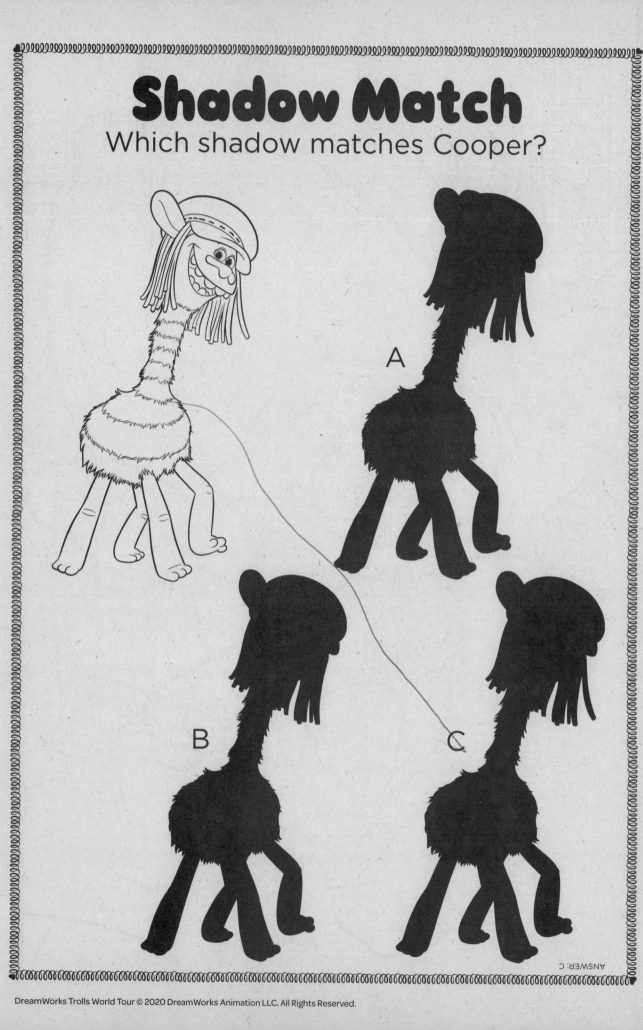

A

B

C

ANSWER: C

Secret Message

Use the key to decipher
the secret message.

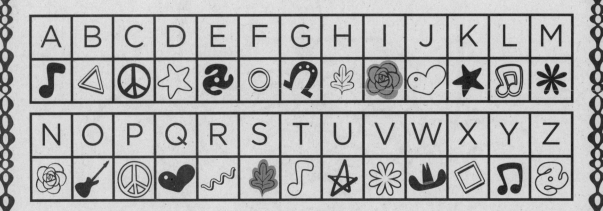

M U S I C

I S

e n e r g y

Dot-to-Dot

Go dot-to-dot to finish the picture of King Thrash!

DRAW

Poppy and her friends are Pop Trolls.
They live in Trolls Village and love pop music.
Draw yourself as a pop star!

Interlock

Complete the puzzle by using
the words from the list.

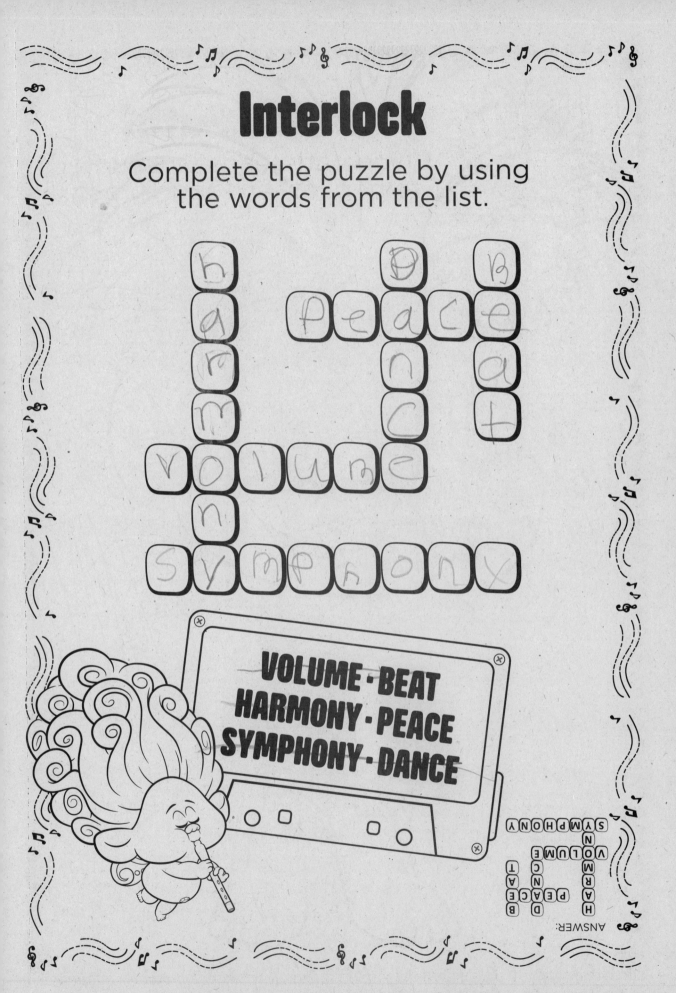

VOLUME · BEAT
HARMONY · PEACE
SYMPHONY · DANCE

Which Path?

Which path leads Queen Barb to her Father, King Thrash?

A

B

C

Your Answer

ANSWER: C

A-MAZE-ING JOURNEY

Help Poppy make her way to the strings!

FINISH

START

ANSWER:

MISSING PIECE

Find the missing piece of the image and finish the drawing of Riff!

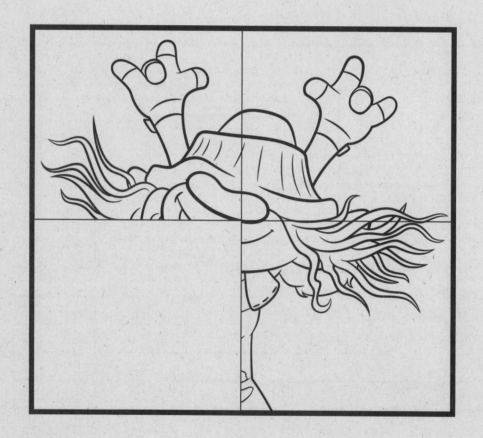

1

2

3

LET'S DRAW!

Trace the gray lines to finish the drawing of the cherub and Pennywhistle!

TRANSFER

Using the paths, transfer the letters into the circles below to unscramble the word.

D E M O Y L

Troll Match

Which two pictures of Guy Diamond ard Tiny Diamond are the same?

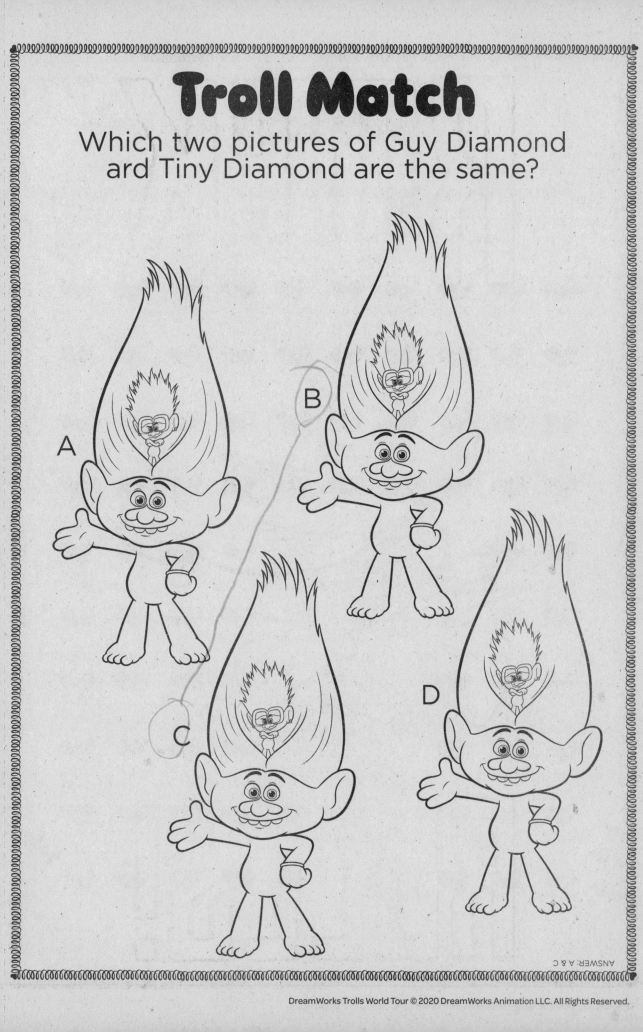

SQUARES

Taking turns, connect a line from one heart to another. Whoever makes the line that completes the square puts his or her initial in the square. The person with the most squares at the end of the game wins!